Kit and Kaboodle

VISIT
THE FARM

By Michelle Portice
Art by Mitch Mortimer

HIGHLIGHTS PRESS
Honesdale, Pennsylvania

Stories + Puzzles = Reading Success!

Dear Parents,

Highlights Puzzle Readers are an innovative approach to learning to read that combines puzzles and stories to build motivated, confident readers.

Developed in collaboration with reading experts, the stories and puzzles are seamlessly integrated so that readers are encouraged to read the story, solve the puzzles, and then read the story again. This helps increase vocabulary and reading fluency and creates a satisfying reading experience for any kind of learner. In addition, solving Hidden Pictures puzzles fosters important reading and learning skills such as:

- shape and letter recognition
- sound-letter relationships
- visual discrimination
- logic
- flexible thinking
- sequencing

With high-interest stories, humorous characters, and trademark puzzles, Highlights Puzzle Readers offer a winning combination for inspiring young learners to love reading.

This is Kit.

This is Kaboodle.

They love to **travel**. You can help them on each **adventure**.

As you read the story, find the objects in each **Hidden Pictures** puzzle.

Then check the **Packing List** on pages 30–31 to make sure you found everything.

Happy reading!

Kit and Kaboodle want
to bake a dessert.

"What should we bake?"
asks Kaboodle.

"My favorite dessert is pie," says Kit.

"Let's make an apple pie!"
says Kaboodle.

"That is a great idea!" says Kit.

"We have flour, butter, salt, sugar, and spices," says Kaboodle.

"There is just one thing we are missing."

"Apples!" says Kit.

"Do you know where
we can get the best apples ever?"
asks Kaboodle.

"Where?" asks Kit.

"At the farm down the road!"
says Kaboodle.

"Today is a great day to go to the farm," says Kit. "Let's get ready!"

Kit packs a few things.

Kaboodle packs a few things. Then he packs more things.

"I hope I don't forget anything," says Kaboodle.

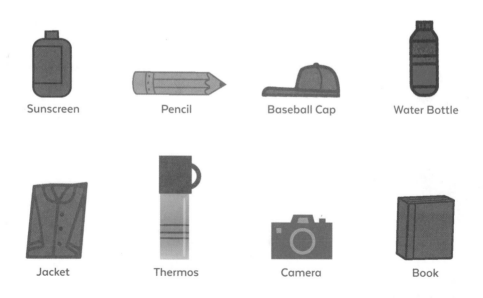

Sunscreen   Pencil   Baseball Cap   Water Bottle

Jacket   Thermos   Camera   Book

STUFF JUNK

TOYS

9

Kit and Kaboodle arrive at the farm.

"We need to get apples," says Kit.
"But look at all the fun things we can do!"

"I've always wanted to go
through a corn maze," says Kaboodle.

"The maze is on our way
to the apples," says Kit. "Let's try it!"

"There are a lot of turns in here,"
says Kit. "I hope we don't lose our way!"

"I've packed a few things
to keep us on track," says Kaboodle.

He looks in his backpack.

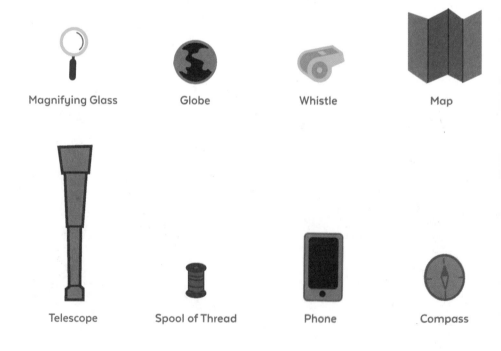

Magnifying Glass   Globe   Whistle   Map

Telescope   Spool of Thread   Phone   Compass

"We made it out!" says Kit.

"That was fun," says Kaboodle.
"I'm glad we did the maze."

"Do you smell that?" asks Kit.

"It smells like doughnuts!" says Kaboodle.

"We can take a quick snack break," says Kaboodle.

"Fresh doughnuts are the best," says Kit.
"But they can be messy."

"Don't worry!" says Kaboodle.
"I brought some things we can use to stay clean."

He looks in his backpack.

Plate   Sink   Bar of Soap   Knife

Bib   Tablecloth   Napkin   Fork

DOUGHNUTS

TOTAL $2.42

"Yum!" says Kit.

"Those doughnuts were delicious."

"On to the apples," says Kaboodle.

"Look, it's a hayride!" says Kit.

"Maybe we can go for one ride," says Kaboodle.

"The farm looks beautiful from here," says Kaboodle.

"It does," says Kit. "But I'm starting to get cold."

"Not a problem!" says Kaboodle. "I packed some things to help us keep warm."

He looks in his backpack.

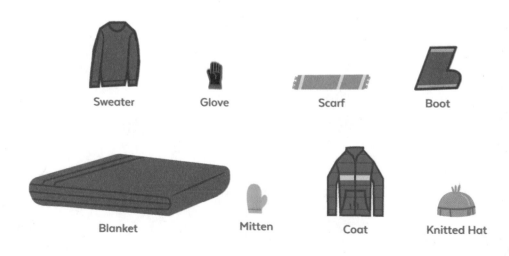

Sweater   Glove   Scarf   Boot

Blanket   Mitten   Coat   Knitted Hat

"Look!" says Kit.
"The hayride dropped us
at the apple orchard."

"There are so many kinds of apples,"
says Kaboodle.

APPLE
BASKETS
HERE

"Those green apples are great for apple pie," says Kit.

"Let's pick them," says Kaboodle.

"These apples look so good," says Kaboodle. "It will be hard not to pick too many!"

"The farmer gave us this basket to fill," says Kit. "We may need something else to hold the extra apples."

"I have something to help us hold the extra apples," says Kaboodle.

He looks in his backpack.

Fanny Pack

Duffel Bag

Laundry Basket

Shopping Cart

Purse

Suitcase

Shopping Bag

Tote Bag

"These apples are going to make a great pie," says Kaboodle.

"Let's go home and start baking!" says Kit.

At home, Kit and Kaboodle make their pie.

Kit rolls out the pie crust.

Kaboodle cuts the apples for the filling.

They put the pie in the oven.

"The pie is ready," says Kit.

"It is delicious!" says Kaboodle.
"We picked perfect apples."

"Going to the farm was a great idea,"
says Kit. "We did so many fun things."

"Where should we go on our next trip?"
asks Kaboodle.

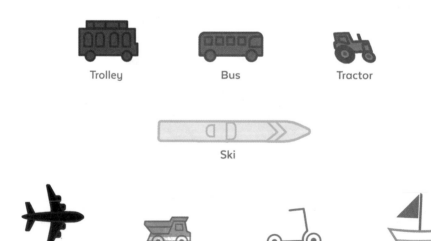

Trolley   Bus   Tractor

Ski

Airplane   Dump Truck   Scooter   Sailboat

Did you find all the things Kit and

 Airplane

 Bar of Soap

 Baseball Cap

 Bib

 Camera

 Coat

 Compass

 Duffel Bag

Glove

 Jacket

 Knife

 Knitted Hat

 Napkin

 Pencil

 Phone

 Plate

 Shopping Bag

 Shopping Cart

 Sink

 Ski

 Tablecloth

 Telescope

 Thermos

 Tote Bag

Kaboodle packed for their trip?

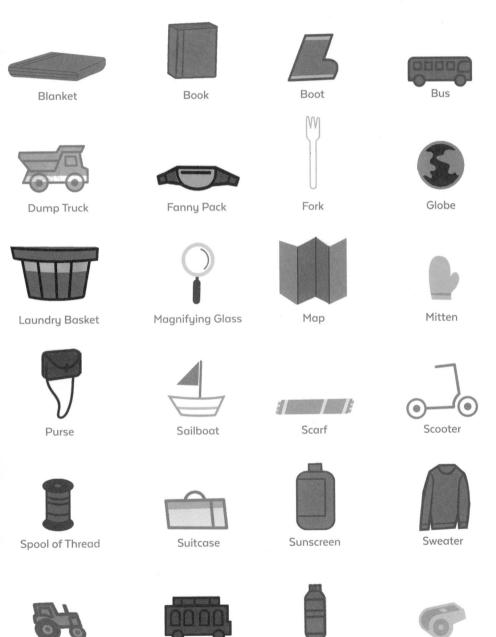

Blanket

Book

Boot

Bus

Dump Truck

Fanny Pack

Fork

Globe

Laundry Basket

Magnifying Glass

Map

Mitten

Purse

Sailboat

Scarf

Scooter

Spool of Thread

Suitcase

Sunscreen

Sweater

Tractor

Trolley

Water Bottle

Whistle

For information about permission to reprint selections from this book,
please contact permissions@highlights.com.

Published by Highlights Press
815 Church Street
Honesdale, Pennsylvania 18431
ISBN (paperback): 978-1-64472-474-3
ISBN (hardcover): 978-1-64472-475-0
ISBN (ebook): 978-1-64472-476-7

Library of Congress Control Number: 2021938014
Manufactured in Melrose Park, IL, USA
Mfg. 09/2021

First edition
Visit our website at Highlights.com.
10 9 8 7 6 5 4 3 2 1

This book has been officially leveled with both the F&P Text Level
Gradient™ Leveling System and the Lexile® Text Measure.

For assistance in the preparation of this book, the editors would like
to thank Vanessa Maldonado, MSEd, MS Literacy Ed. K–12, Reading/LA
Consultant Cert., K–5 Literacy Instructional Coach; and Gina Shaw.